Lalaloopsy™
Sew Magical! Sew Cute!

Star of the Show

SCHOLASTIC INC.

by Kris Marvin Hughes

ISBN 978-0-545-62985-0

10 9 8 7 6 5 4 3 2 1

14 15 16 17 18 19/0

Printed in the U.S.A.
First printing, August 2014

40

"This year's Sparkle and Shine Party has to be extra sparkly," Jewel Sparkles told Pix E. Flutters. The two friends were at Jewel's house. "We need sparkly costumes and sparkly snacks."

"Tippy Tumblelina and Crumbs Sugar Cookie can do that," said Pix E.

Just then, Spot Splatter Splash arrived. "Here's the artwork for the show," she said, turning on a spotlight.

"Wow, SO sparkly!" exclaimed Jewel and Pix E.

"That gives me an idea for the grand finale," said Pix E.

"**W**hat if we have something sparkly fly across the night sky?" continued Pix E.

"Yes! Someone can dress up as a shooting star!" cried Jewel. "It has to be someone who likes to fly and is sparkly. Who do we know like that?"

"Me!" cried Pix E., tossing fairy dust into the air.

While Pix E. was preparing for the finale, Jewel went to visit Crumbs.

"Could you bake sparkly cupcakes for the party?" Jewel asked.

"No problem," said Crumbs. "All I need is—"

Before Crumbs could finish, Mouse brought her sugar, flour, butter, and eggs.

"Good job, Mouse! You can be my Official Pastry Assistant," said Crumbs. "Let's get started!"

Meanwhile, Pix E. was on her way to see Peanut Big Top. She needed Peanut's help with the finale.

"I'm going to fly above the crowd as a shooting star at the Sparkle and Shine Party, and . . . well . . . I don't know how to fly," Pix E. said.

"But you have wings," said Peanut.
"Yes, but they're not real wings," Pix E. explained.
"Okay, safety first!" said Peanut. She gave Pix E. some padding.
Next, Peanut wrapped a rope around Pix E. Then Elephant lifted
her into the air.

"Peanut, thank you for making my dream come true. I've always wanted to fly," said Pix E.

But as Elephant pulled Pix E. higher, she got scared.

"I think I want to come down now," Pix E. said nervously.

"How can I be a star if I'm afraid of heights?" Pix E. asked. "Don't worry, Pix E. Everyone's afraid of something," said Peanut. "Go see Bea Spells-a-Lot. Maybe she has a book about getting over fears."

"I have exactly the books you need," Bea told Pix E. But instead of giving Pix E. books to read, Bea put them on the grass. "Please stand on this book," said Bea. Pix E. did it easily. Then Pix E. stepped onto the next book. It was a little higher off the ground.

"You did it!" cried Bea. "Now for the next book."

By now, Pix E. was getting dizzy. "Maybe I shouldn't have volunteered to be a shooting star," she said.

"Perhaps Dot Starlight can help," said Bea. "She knows lots about stars."

"Dot, can you help me?" asked Pix E.
"I have just the thing," said Dot.
Dot gave Pix E. extra-large wings and put her in front of a fan.

Pix E.'s wings and dress fluttered in the breeze.
"Pix E., you're doing great! Let's turn up the power," suggested Dot.
But now the wind was too strong. It knocked Pix E. over!

"Firefly, I've tried everything. I don't want to disappoint Jewel, but I think I need to tell her the truth," Pix E. said sadly. "There isn't going to be a grand finale."

ix E. went to see Jewel. She was trying on party dresses with Tippy Tumblelina.

"Jewel, I have to tell you something," Pix E. said.

"Hold that thought," said Jewel. "Come see the shooting-star costume Tippy made for you!"

Tippy pulled a rope, and out swung a dress.

Pix E. couldn't believe her eyes. It was the sparkliest, most beautiful dress she had ever seen. And the way Jewel's closet worked gave Pix E. an idea, too!

"What did you want to talk about, Pix E.?" Jewel asked.
"Oh . . . uh, I wanted to say how excited I am for the show.
See you tonight!" Pix E. exclaimed.
Pix E. finally knew how to make her dream come true!

The time had come for the Sparkle and Shine Party.
"I'd like to thank everyone who made this party happen," said Jewel. "Spot, Crumbs, Tippy, and, of course, myself for having this fabulous idea."

All the Lalaloopsy were amazed! They had never seen anything so sparkly.

"And now, the moment you've all been waiting for — the shooting star!" said Jewel.

Pix E. glided against the night sky. Her face shone proudly as she soared through the air.

"Firefly, I'm doing it! I'm really flying!" cried Pix E.

Up in a tree, Peanut pulled a rope — just like the one in Jewel's closet. Pix E. swung from side to side, just as Tippy's dress had.

"*Whoa!*" the crowd cheered. "That's amazing!"

It was the most spectacular party Lalaloopsy Land had ever seen!

Later that night, Pix E. was happy to be home. "Firefly, where should I hang this sparkly star from the party?"

Firefly flew to a nail high up on the wall.

"That is the best place," Pix E. agreed. She hung the star, wobbling a bit. "Okay, that's high enough for today!"